Love Puppies

WE'RE HERE TO HELP!

Changing Tunes

JaNay Brown-Wood

SCHOLASTIC INC.

To Poursha, Denise, Myesha,
and all of my many wonderful cousins.
I love you all so very much!

Copyright © 2024 by JaNay Brown-Wood.

Interior illustrations by Eric Proctor, © 2024 Scholastic Inc.

All rights reserved. Published by Scholastic Inc., *Publishers since 1920.* SCHOLASTIC and associated logos are trademarks and/or registered trademarks of Scholastic Inc.

The publisher does not have any control over and does not assume any responsibility for author or third-party websites or their content.

No part of this publication may be reproduced, stored in a retrieval system, or transmitted in any form or by any means, electronic, mechanical, photocopying, recording, or otherwise, without written permission of the publisher. For information regarding permission, write to Scholastic Inc., Attention: Permissions Department, 557 Broadway, New York, NY 10012.

This book is a work of fiction. Names, characters, places, and incidents are either the product of the author's imagination or are used fictitiously, and any resemblance to actual persons, living or dead, business establishments, events, or locales is entirely coincidental.

ISBN 978-1-339-04216-9

10 9 8 7 6 5 4 3 2 1   24 25 26 27 28

Printed in the U.S.A.   40

First printing 2024

Book design by Omou Barry

Decorative design border art © Shutterstock.com

Fall in love with each paw-fectly sweet adventure!

TABLE OF CONTENTS

Chapter 1
Unsung Plans

"Did you hear that?" asked Noodles as her ears

focused in on a sound from somewhere in the Love

Puppy Doghouse. Or did it come from outside?

"I didn't hear anything," said Clyde. He

was sprawled out on the carpet with a bowl of

doggie treats balanced on his Shar-Pei tummy.

"Me either," responded Barkley. He and Rosie rolled a ball back and forth across the floor of the living room, where the Love Puppy team sat and waited.

"I'm sure I heard something," said Noodles. "I'll go check!"

Noodles jumped onto her feet, wagging her tail excitedly. She hurried out of the living room and down the hall to the big window beside the front door. Noodles placed both paws on the windowpane and peeked out.

"Is she here?" called Rosie, her voice carrying down the hallway.

Nope. Nobody was there.

Waiting was super hard. Especially when your very most favorite cousin was on her way for a visit.

Noodles dropped back down to all fours and padded back into the living room.

"No sign of Curlicue yet," she said, answering Rosie's question. A rain cloud was beginning to collect over her head. Even though the Love Puppies were a team of magical puppies, not even their magic could make Cousin Curli come any sooner.

"She'll be here at any moment, pretty pup," said Rosie, with a smile on her adorable golden retriever face. "No need to worry."

Noodles's rain cloud grew a little bigger, as if filling up with raindrops ready to downpour on top of her little labradoodle head. This was Noodles's power—she could control elements of weather as easy as one, two, three. She could also detect strong emotions, which caused her nose to glow a beautiful orange. And that's just what her nose did at that very moment as the rain cloud above her head continued to grow.

Rosie eyed the expanding cloud and the tears welling up in Noodles's eyes.

"What's taking her so long?" Noodles howled, flopping down onto her belly.

"Why don't you tell us what you have planned for

her visit?" said Rosie. "That'll take your mind off of the waiting."

Rosie's words caused a rainbow to burst through the rain cloud. Its shimmering colors made the room fill with lovely light, casting colors over the hanging banners that displayed animated versions of each of the Love Puppies. The banner-pups yipped and danced on their fabrics. They always kept the real Love Puppies company from their banners that hung from the ceiling in the living room.

And Noodles's tail got to wagging happily, again. "So many things, Rosie-Posie!" said Noodles.

"Tell us!" said Clyde, now sitting up, his own tail flailing with enthusiasm.

"Well, first, we're going to hit the pool for some fun in the sun. Curli *loves* a summertime dip, especially when she can tan her fur. Then maybe we can play a game of Pass the Beachball-Barkley . . ."

"Sounds like my kind of game!" said Barkley. His tiny dachshund body sparkled as he morphed from a puppy into a purple beachball with light and dark stripes. That was Barkley's magic: He could change into just about anything, and even camouflage with the things around him, or dis-appear completely.

Beachball-Barkley bounced across the floor. Then it took to the air as Barkley morphed back into his puppy body and landed on his feet like a graceful gymnast, with his tiny front legs stretched up above his head.

"That was a perfect ten," said Rosie with a laugh. She tossed roses and rose petals into the air so they showered over Barkley as he bowed. Rosie had flower magic—she could grow plants and flowers with ease. The other pups clapped and cheered at Barkley's perfect landing.

"What else, what else!" asked Clyde.

"Then I thought we'd watch the sunset and maybe you can cook up your tasty Sausage S'mores, Clydie. The ones with the dog biscuits and cheese and brown sugar bacon."

"Paw-some idea!" said Clyde. He somersaulted

through the air and did a jig on the ceiling. Clyde had the power of flight, but he could also identify tastes in the air. And he was an excellent cook!

"This all sounds like so much fun," said Rosie. "It's going to be such a wonderful time!"

"If only she'd get here already, I can't wait to—" A ringing doorbell stopped Noodles midsentence.

"She's here! She's here!" called all the puppies as they dashed from the living room to the front door.

Noodles opened the door and a white toy poodle burst through wearing star-shaped sunglasses, a bright scarf around her neck, and all her toenails painted a sparkly teal to match the glasses and scarf.

"I'm heeeeeeerrrrreeeeee!" sang the poodle,

holding the note. Her beautiful voice filled up the hallway, dazzling the puppies' eardrums. Her voice slid from a low note all the way up to a high note, which she continued to hold without taking a breath. "I. Am. Here!" she crooned. Then she took a bow.

"Bravo!" yelled Barkley.

"Beautiful," called Rosie as she clapped.

"Isn't she pup-tastic?!" Noodles said with a proud glow.

The pups charged Curlicue and covered her with puppy kisses. All the happiness and love filling up the front door hallway caused Noodles's nose to shine full blast, as well as Rosie's bright heart,

Clyde's tummy, and Barkley's whole body. The shining light from the Love Puppy team bounced off the walls and ceiling like a disco ball spinning in a dance hall.

Curlicue's eyes grew wide. "Wowzies!" she called. "I don't remember you all being able to do that."

"Yeah," said Noodles. "Our powers have gotten stronger since the last time we saw you." She and the pups had visited Curli many times, but this was Curli's first visit to the Doghouse.

Rosie took three deep breaths and then her shimmering heart dimmed. Clyde and Barkley did the same, dimming their own shining, too.

"That's simply amazing!" said Curli.

"No more amazing than your voice!" said Rosie. "I could listen to you sing all day!"

"Thank you, doll," responded Curli. "But having magical powers must be the best thing ever!"

Noodles's nose still glowed from the excitement in the room, even though she had already taken many deep breaths. "I'm still working on getting mine under control," she said with her cheeks a little pink.

"Well, Noodly-Doodly, that's faaaaaaancy," Curli sang.

Noodles hugged Curli again. "I've missed you, cousin. Let's get you all situated. You're going to stay in my room. Come on!"

Each of the pups picked up one of Curli's four bags and followed Noodles to one of the back rooms.

"We have so many things planned," Noodles said, bouncing back and forth in her room. "Like Barkley Beachball and swimming and tanning and . . ."

Just then, a loud buzzing sound filled the air. Each of the pups sighed deeply.

"Do you all hear that?" Curli asked. "What's that sound?"

While the answer wasn't clear to Curli, it definitely was for the Love Puppies. That was the sound of ruined plans!

Chapter 2
Mission Magnolia

"Well, let's go, Pups," said Rosie as she turned and

hurried out of Noodles's room. Barkley and Clyde

followed close behind.

"We've got to go, too," said Noodles. "Come on,

you can join us."

Curli trailed Noodles as they jogged down the hallway and into the living room. Curli stopped. There, the Crystal Bone blinked brightly—pink, orange, purple, and blue—and levitated off the ground as it buzzed.

"Wowzies!" said Curli, once again. She eyed the giant, floating crystalline bone and the metal platform it was attached to. Finally, it stopped buzzing and blinking and landed back on the ground, right beside Rosie.

"Let's see what the Bone has for us today," Rosie said. She placed her paws onto the Bone's surface and closed her eyes as her paw pads glowed pink. Light and words projected onto the ceiling:

NAME: MAGNOLIA HALVERSTON
Age: Seven
Grade: Second
Problem: Feeling left out because of a brand-new baby brother

Curli watched as each of the puppies looked up. But when she looked up, all she saw was the white of the painted ceiling.

"What are you all looking at?" Curli asked.

"You can't see it?" asked Clyde, scratching his head. None of the Love Puppies ever had a hard time seeing the Crystal Bone's projections before.

"Nothing but the ceiling," said Curli.

"Oh," said Rosie. "It's because without the Love Puppy magic, you can't see the messages. No worries. We'll tell you what we see. This is Mission Magnolia. She's a seven-year-old with a new baby brother, and I don't think it's going so well."

Rosie pulled her paws from the Bone and cupped them in front of her. A pink hologram shined on her glowing paws. Three people appeared: A toddler-aged Magnolia, her mom, and her mommy. All three played together smiling and laughing. Mom and Mommy held Magnolia's hands and swung her as they laughed. "Go, Maggie, go!" said Mommy.

"Hmmm," said Rosie. "Interesting."

"What? What is it?" said Curli, who was now so close to Rosie's upturned paws that the tip of Curli's nose was almost touching Rosie's puppy paw pads.

"It's a little Magnolia and her mommies," said Noodles. "They are happy and having a blast."

The scene playing out on Rosie's paws shifted, and now Magnolia sat beside Mommy and her giant belly. Mom rubbed the belly with a smile, and Magnolia leaned over and kissed Mommy's belly gently. "Can't wait to meet you, baby brother," said Magnolia.

"Magnolia's mommy has a baby in her tummy, now and everybody seems so excited," said Barkley, still not taking his eyes off the hologram scene.

Then the hologram blinked brightly, and the image shifted back to the ceiling as the next scene played out. A red-faced Magnolia leaned out of her bedroom door. Her fists were balled up tight and tears spilled from her eyes. "I hate having a baby brother," she screamed.

The pups gasped in shock and Noodles's nose turned on full-bright again.

"Oh no!" whimpered Clyde.

"What?" whispered Curli. "What is it?"

"It's not going very well at all," said Rosie in a gloomy voice.

"You don't even love me anymore!" screamed Magnolia. "I wish he was never born!" She slammed the door and the hologram burned out.

The pups sat in absolute silence. A new hologram buzzed up on the surface of the Bone. A baby cried loudly in the background in another room, and Magnolia sat on her bed, holding her knees, rocking herself gently, and crying.

"Bone tells me that this is Magnolia right now," said Rosie.

The pups broke into sobs and huddled together.

"What? What did it show? What happened now?" Curli asked, watching the pups hug one another and cry.

"It's really bad," sniffled Noodles. "Magnolia no longer feels loved and her heart is broken because of it."

"She feels left out and all alone," said Rosie. "And she's going to need our help."

But at that moment, Curli could understand the feeling. What happened to hanging out with her favorite cousin? And how could a completely unmagical puppy like her help out when the other puppies already knew exactly what to do?

With the Love Puppies busy helping this human girl feel loved, who was going to help Curli feel like she mattered, too?

Chapter 3
A Pup and Her Siblings

Noodles reached her paw out to Curli. "Come here, cousin," she said. All the other pups sniffled as they made a spot for her.

Curli joined in the huddle, looking around the circle of teary-eyed puppies and Noodles's beaming nose.

"Where do we even start?" asked Rosie. "I've never had a little brother or sister."

"Me neither," said Clyde.

Barkley nodded in agreement.

"Feeling bad because of a new sibling—I've never had to deal with something like that, either," said Noodles.

"Well, *I* have," said Curli. "I have eleven little brother and sister pups!"

"That's true! All my other cousins," said Noodle. "You definitely have experience there!"

"It's not as hard as it may seem—at least it wasn't for me," Curli said. "I mean, yeah, puplings bug you. And they take your stuff. Oh, and eat all your favorite beef gravy-flavored kibble."

"That's paw-ful!" said Clyde with disbelief in his voice.

"True. But once you get over them bugging you all the time, having puplings is kinda cool," Curli said. "You always have somepuppy to play with. And somepuppy who gets your silly jokes and will laugh, even if nopuppy else gets them."

"But how does that help a human like Magnolia?" asked Barkley. "Her brother is still a brand-new baby. He can't talk or laugh at jokes yet. All he does is cry. And poop."

Each of the pups crinkled up their nose at Barkley's words.

"I'm pretty sure Magnolia doesn't like that very much," added Clyde. "How could a new baby like that know how to stop bugging a big sister like her?"

"All good thoughts and questions," said Rosie. "Maybe we need to go see Magnolia in action at home. Maybe that'll give us an idea of how to help her cope with this new baby brother."

"Can I come, too?" asked Curli. She didn't want to be left behind while the Love Puppies went out and explored together and had a whole bunch of fun.

"Hmmm, can you come?" Rosie wondered aloud. "We've never taken a nonmagical puppy with us through the Love Puppy Doggie Door before."

"I don't know if you'd like it much, Curli-Girly," said Noodles. She could tell Rosie was worried about something going wrong. "Wouldn't you rather take a dip in the doggie pool?"

"Nah," said Curli. "I just got my fur fluffed." She turned her head to show her perfectly fluffy poodle curls.

"You could relax in the library," Noodles said, trying again.

"Just finished two books on the way over: *Poodles Just Wanna Have Fun* and *A Tale of Two Poodles*— which I would recommend if you are looking for a good book to read," said Curli.

"Maybe you can whip something up in the

kitchen? Or explore Rosie's garden? Or the puppy playroom?" Noodles pushed on.

"If I didn't know better, Noodly-Doodly, I would think you didn't want me to come." Curli's eyebrows raised high on her face.

"No, that's not it at all—" Noodles began.

"It's okay," interjected Rosie. "I think we can give it a try. Plus, time to help Magnolia is slipping away. Are we ready, Pups?"

Curli and the others nodded.

"Okay. Paws in! With the Power of Love, anything is paw-sible. Love Puppies, go!"

With the glowing of their paw pads and a *whoosh*, the spinning Doggie Door portal opened up to transport them from the Doghouse to their destination: Magnolia's home.

Clyde jumped in first. Then Barkley.

"Come on, Curli," said Noodles as she took Curli's paw. "We can go together." Into the portal they jumped, followed by Rosie.

As the puppies twisted and turned, Curli screamed the whole time from entry to exit. Her word *HEEEEEEELLLLLLLLPPPPPPPP* sounded as if she were singing onstage at a world-class opera.

"Curli's really got pipes on her," said Barkley, rubbing his sore ears once they landed on the lush grass of Magnolia's front lawn. The all hid behind a giant tree.

"I think I'm gonna be sick," cried Curli. "That was simply awful! Does anypuppy else see dancing paw-prints swirling around your heads? I don't think I can even walk." Curli placed the back of her paw onto her forehead.

Barkley morphed his body into a fan and sent cool air over Curli's fur.

Rosie eyed Noodles with concern on her face.

"Don't worry, Rosie," said Noodles. "I'll stay back with her to make sure she's okay. You pups go."

"You sure?" asked Rosie.

"Yeah. I mean she's *my* guest," said Noodles. "I'll take care of her so you can investigate. You pups fill me in later about what you find."

"But . . ." started Clyde, his ears beginning to wiggle with worry. ". . . but what if we miss something Noodles would have seen? What if we need her wind or rain? What if . . ."

"Whoa, Clydie," said Rosie, patting him gently between his ears. "Big breaths, boy. Big breaths."

Clyde took some deep breaths to calm down.

Noodles was paw-tastic at noticing little details. And her weather abilities always came in handy. The team did have reason to worry.

Rosie took her own big breath. "It'll be okay," she said. "She'll just be right here if we need her. Right, pretty pup?"

"Right," answered Noodles, who was now petting Curli's fur softly.

But even Rosie's own words didn't help the worry at all.

"Come on, Pups. We'd better go," she finally said, trying to hide the concern in her voice. And the three pups scurried off, leaving Noodles and Curli behind in the shade of the huge oak tree.

Chapter 4
Oh Brother!

The Love Puppies—minus Noodles—hurried toward the house. Rosie used her magic to grow tall blades of grass that hid them as they moved across the lawn.

"Shhh, do you hear that?" asked Rosie. She

stopped in her tracks and perked her ears up straight.

The soft voice of a girl carried on the wind.

"I think that's her," whispered Rosie. "Sounds like she's this way. Let's go."

With Rosie in the lead, the pups dashed over to the backyard fence. Rosie hopped onto Clyde's back as Barkley morphed into Bumblebee-Barkley. They flew over the fence with no problem at all and landed beside one of the walls of a backyard shed.

"There she is," said Clyde as they stacked their puppy heads and looked around a corner.

Magnolia sat on a swing set with another girl.

"It's the worst, Tatiana," said Magnolia. "It's like my moms don't even know I'm here anymore. Like they don't even love me."

"That can't be true, Maggie," said Tatiana. "They're just a little busy right now. What did you say Benji has again?"

"Colic," answered Magnolia. "It means he cries *all the time*. Just cries and cries and cries. And then they forget all about me."

"Have you told your moms how you feel?" Tatiana asked.

"Why would I? All they see is that baby." Magnolia kicked at a rock on the ground, causing her swing to jiggle just a bit. The two sat in silence.

Almost as if on cue, a baby's cry cut through the quiet, even though the windows and doors were closed. Magnolia looked toward the house, a frown deepening across her face.

"Can I come live with you?" she said.

"It'll get easier, Maggie. I promise," said Tatiana. "When my little sisters were born, it was hard at first. But after some time, it got much better."

Benji's cries got louder as Mom opened the sliding glass door and poked her head out.

"Mags," she said, "dinner is ready. Time to come eat. Have a good evening, Tati."

"Good night, Mrs. Halverston." Tatiana waved as Mom closed the door and went back inside.

"You sure I can't just come live with you?" Magnolia asked again. The girls stood and gave each other a hug.

"I'll see you tomorrow, Maggie. Bye."

"Bye."

Tatiana approached the hidden puppies and let herself out of the backyard fence.

Magnolia took a big breath, held it, and then went in.

"Come on," said Rosie. The pups dashed over to the sliding glass door and looked inside.

The living room was covered in baby stuff: baby clothes folded on couches. Bags of baby diapers. Baby toys, bottles, and burping blankets.

"It looks like a baby-stuff explosion in there," said Clyde.

"There they are," whispered Barkley.

Past the living room was a dining room table where the moms sat. Mommy held Baby Benji, who wiggled and fussed but had quieted down. Mommy patted him gently while holding him at her shoulder.

Magnolia leaned over toward Benji and wiggled her finger at him.

"That's nice," said Rosie. "She looks like she's trying to like him."

Then Magnolia picked up a clean binky and tried to put it into his mouth. Benji jerked and his hand hit hers, which sent the binky flying. Benji began crying loudly again. At that, Magnolia stood up and stomped into the kitchen, rolling her eyes.

"It takes time, Maggie," said Mommy, standing and bouncing Benji while patting him. "He's just getting used to everything. You have to be patient with him."

"Can I eat in my room?" Maggie asked, making her voice louder than Benji's cries. She stood in the kitchen doorway, holding a plate of steaming food.

Mommy and Mom looked at each other.

"I have a headache, so . . ." Magnolia trailed off.

"Go ahead, honey," said Mommy.

"Can I join you?" asked Mom.

"No, that's okay. I just want to be alone."

"Okay, Mags," Mom said. "I'll be in there to tuck you in in a bit."

"Like you did last night?" Magnolia said with hurt in her voice.

Mom sighed. "Mags, I apologized for falling asleep last night when I was putting Benji to bed. How about this: I'll read you two stories tonight to make up for it."

Magnolia shrugged her shoulders and walked down the hall and out of view.

"Which room is hers?" asked Rosie, looking at Barkley and Clyde. "You two go scope it out on the top floors. I'll check the windows down here."

A short while later, Barkley called, "Up here. I see her!" Clyde swooped down to get Rosie, and the three huddled on a second-floor balcony, looking in at a lonely Magnolia. She sat on her bed, pushing her food around with her fork.

"She's not even going to taste it?" asked Clyde, his mouth watering at the smell of the baked chicken. He could taste it as the smell wafted on the air and through the crack in the balcony door.

"I don't think she is," answered Rosie.

Magnolia put her plate of uneaten food down onto her bedside table and changed into her pajamas in the bathroom. The pups watched as she brushed her teeth and sat back on her bed.

"It's not even night yet," said Clyde, looking at the sunlit sky.

"And going to bed on an empty tummy is *never* a good thing," added Rosie.

Suddenly, Baby Benji's cries echoed down the hall.

"Ugggh," growled Magnolia. She scooped up a pillow from her bed and slammed it down onto her comforter. Then she began to bang her fists into it. "Babies are the worst!" she said, each word punctuated with her punches. "Babies are the worst. Even when you try to help them, babies are the worst."

Magnolia's pain and sadness filled the room as she chanted the words over and over again. The chants changed to tears and she pulled the pillow up to her face and sobbed into it.

"If Noodles was here right now," said Barkley sadly, "her nose would be lighting up the whole world."

The puppies watched as Magnolia pulled back her bedsheets and climbed under her covers. She pulled the blanket over her head, plugged her ears with her fingers, and sang herself to sleep, the words *babies are the worst* turning from a chant to a whisper, and then to silence and soft breaths.

Rosie, Barkley, and Clyde looked at one another. Just then, a rustle came from below the balcony.

"Pups," called a whispered voice. "Are you all up there?"

The team rushed to the edge of the balcony and looked down at Noodles, who looked up at them.

"Any luck finding out something new?" she asked.

"It's heartbreaking, Noodles," cried Rosie as she and the other pups whimpered.

"Oh no!" said Noodles from below. "Come down, Pups."

Magic Carpet-Barkley flew Rosie and Clyde down to Noodles, and the puppies hugged one another close.

"This is a hard one," said Barkley.

"It's okay, Pups. We'll figure it out," said Noodles.

"But it sounds like you've gotten all you need for now. Let's go get Curli and go home."

With Magnolia's heart bursting with so much sadness, the pups were going to have to figure something out soon.

Really, *really* soon. But what?

Chapter 5
Dinner and a Show

Back at the Doghouse, the pups sat down for dinner with an added placemat for Curli.

The sadness of the day left Clyde uninspired to cook something special, so they all gobbled down puppy kibble with a side of beef bones. Their dinnertime was glum and depressed, as if one of Noodles's clouds was shadowing them in gloom.

"It was so hard to watch, Noodle," said Clyde. "She didn't even eat her tasty-looking dinner."

"Not one bite," said Rosie. "And she even tried to help Benji with a binky, but he didn't want it."

"Yeah, and the night before," added Barkley, "one of Magnolia's moms fell asleep without tucking her in or reading her a story."

"Did her mom come and tuck her in before you pups left?" asked Noodles.

"Uh-uh," said Barkley, shaking his head. "No moms had come by before you called us."

"Oh no. And no one offered to eat dinner with

her?" Noodles asked, trying her best to get a full idea of all that happened.

"Yeah, her mom did. But Magnolia said she wanted to be alone," said Clyde between bites of beef bone.

"This *is* sad," said Noodles, looking down at her own untouched meal.

"Enough of that," said Curli, cutting the sad silence with her voice. "Want to hear a new song I wrote?"

"In a second, Curli-Girly," said Noodles. "How did the moms seem after Magnolia left?"

"Um, I didn't really notice," answered Rosie.

"Me neither," said Barkley.

At that moment, Curli jumped up onto the center of the table, standing on her hind legs, and breaking into song:

"Hey, puppies, hey, puppies.

Wanna know a secret?

I can only tell you one."

Rosie, Clyde, and Barkley looked up at her, smiles creeping across their faces.

"Yeah!" called Clyde. "I want to know a secret. I like secrets."

Curli continued her song, this time, stepping side to side as she sang:

"I know the best way

that a pup can have some fun."

"You do?" said Barkley.

"Yep," said Curli, right before jumping back into

her tune, twirling and dancing on the tabletop:

"You gotta

dance like nopuppy's watching.

You gotta

sing like the world is your microphone.

You gotta

move and groove.

Hey! It's all up to you.

That's how a puppy has fun.

Come on!"

She sang, pulling Rosie, Barkley, and Clyde onto

the table to join and dance with her. They even

joined in on the song, clapping and dancing and laughing.

All except Noodles. She had already missed watching Maggie because of Curli's tummy issues before. And now the fill-in session had gotten cut short by more of Curli's shenanigans.

* * *

Noodles's nose glowed bright with frustration as she watched her puppy team and Curli dance and sing on the table. Clyde did midair somersault dance moves and Barkley morphed into a disco ball, spinning and casting the others in reflective light. Rosie danced with a rose between her teeth.

Just like that, Curli had changed the mood of the room with one of her songs. True, no more gloom or sad hung in the air. But Curli had completely distracted the others from the task at hand.

Noodles closed her eyes and took deep, deep breaths. Her nose dimmed but did not shut off completely.

Noodles climbed down from her seat. "Rosie," she called over their gleeful song, "can you turn on the Mission Monitor, please?"

"Sure thing, pretty pup," Rosie said, jumping down from the table. "Be right back. Don't have too much fun without me!" she said with a smile.

Rosie followed Noodles into the living room, the

happy voices of the other pups filling the air. Rosie stopped at the Crystal Bone.

"You sure you don't want to join us in there, Noodly-Poo?" asked Rosie, "or finish your dinner?"

"I already missed Maggie earlier," said Noodles. "I want to see what I can do to help her."

"Okay. Here you go."

Rosie stood up on her back legs and placed her paws onto the Crystal Bone. "Mission Monitor, please," she said to the Bone.

A long panel opened up in the ceiling and a large television-like screen slowly dropped down. This was the Mission Monitor, another tool used by the Love Puppy team to help kids in need. At Rosie's request, the large screen allowed them to peer into the lives of children who the pups were currently on a mission to help.

The Mission Monitor blinked once, then twice. Finally, Magnolia appeared on the screen, sleeping peacefully with her covers pulled over her head and only her face visible.

Noodles sat down in front of the screen.

"Want me to sit and watch with you?" asked Rosie.

"No, that's okay," Noodles responded, not taking her eyes off the screen. "You go play with the others. I'll just do some watching by myself."

"Well, it's really clear that Maggie feels left out," said Rosie.

"Yeah. I think you are right about that," said Noodles.

Rosie padded over to the hallway and stopped once more. "Don't be gone long. We'll miss you too much."

"Okay, Rosie-Posie," said Noodles.

Rosie bounded out of the room to join the others. Noodles looked after her, still hearing Curli and her team singing loudly from the kitchen.

Maybe Noodles *would* have liked to have Rosie's help. That way, she would not have to figure this out all on her own.

At that moment, a door opened in Magnolia's room and Mom poked her head in.

"Mags," she said softly. She opened the door completely and walked inside. "Mags, are you ready for your bedtime stories? I've got two," she said holding up the books.

Mom's shoulders dropped as she looked at Maggie, fast asleep. She walked over to the untouched food and sighed. Mom then leaned over and kissed Maggie on the forehead.

"Sorry we missed another bedtime story before you fell asleep, kiddo," she whispered to the sleeping Magnolia. "I hope you know how much we love you."

Mom picked up the plate and left, closing the door gently behind her.

"Seems like the moms don't quite know what to do to help Maggie either," Noodles said aloud to herself. "Wait a minute," she said, rubbing her own puppy chin with one of her paws. "Help. Maybe that's the first step to get Maggie pulled back into the family. Giving *her* a way to lend a helping hand. That's it!"

Noodles jumped up onto her feet and ran into the kitchen, yelling, "Pups! Pups! I know what we can do so Maggie will feel better! I know what we can do to help!"

Chapter 6
Help on the Way

When Noodles entered the kitchen, the pups had

moved from the table to the countertop. They sang

at the top of their lungs with Curli front and center

holding a whisk like a microphone. They had also

crafted costumes using dress-up clothes from the

puppy playroom and had painted a sign that said CURLI AND THE LOVE PUPPY BAND. And on the kitchen floor below the countertop stood a bunch of teddy bears and stuffed puppy toys.

"Pups!" Noodles repeated, stepping over the stuffed audience. "I know what we can do to help Maggie!"

The music stopped as all eyes found Noodles.

"You do?" asked Barkley, wiggling his tail. A pirate patch covered his left eye and a banana necktie sat at his throat. He climbed down to meet Noodles.

"I think so," said Noodles.

"Way to go," said Clyde, swooping down to her level, too. He wore an oversized polka-dotted top hat on his head and tap shoes on his hind paws.

Rosie jumped down next, in a frilly pink princess dress and with a tiara on her head.

Noodles couldn't help but laugh at her team of silly-dressed pups.

Curli stayed standing on her hind legs on top of the counter. She wore white go-go boots on her back paws and a big, bright, teal, and oversized bow on her head.

"How can we help her?" asked Rosie. "What's your idea?"

"Well," began Noodles, "it seems like Maggie has a lot of emotions whirling around inside her. That's definitely clear," she said, tapping her nose, which glowed dimly. "She's bugged by the new baby and she's feeling left out."

"I know the feeling," Curli said under her breath. She dropped down to all fours and rolled her eyes.

Noodles continued on, not hearing Curli's words. "Maybe we can give her something *big* to do to help! That can make her feel like she's a part of the family again. That can make her feel like she belongs!"

"Oh yeah," said Rosie. "Like how she tried to help with the binky, but Baby Benji didn't take it."

"Exactly!" said Noodles, her tail wiggle-waggling as if it were a part of Curli and the Love Puppy Band.

"Ooooh, maybe she can make the baby a steak

dinner," said Clyde. "That way, the baby can have a full and happy tummy!"

"That might not work so well, Clydie," said Rosie, "since babies don't have teeth yet and can't chew steaks."

"True," said Clyde. "Plus, I don't know if Maggie even knows how to sear a steak to make it just right." Clyde closed his eyes and pictured sizzling steaks dancing from the stovetop to his mouth. "Yum!"

"Focus, Clydie," giggled Rosie.

"What about helping with cleaning the house?" said Barkley. "They did have a lot of baby stuff all over."

"I'm not sure if that would really help her feel a

part of the family, unless they all did that together," said Noodles.

"Maybe she could help with diapers," said Curli, licking one of her paws. "Babies need diaper changes all the time, right? I know that would really help her moms *and* the baby."

"Great idea, Curli-Girly!" said Noodles, filled up with excitement. "Diapers. A pup-tastic idea!"

Curli smiled at her cousin's words.

"That will definitely give her something to do to help. Come on, Pups," said Noodles, "we need a special Diaper Delivery!"

Chapter 7
Diaper Delivery

The pups hightailed it back to the living room where the Mission Monitor still showed a sleeping Maggie.

"How do we even get diapers to deliver?" asked Clyde.

"I bet there are some already at the house," answered Rosie. "We may have to just go look around a bit to find them."

Just then, a hallway light clicked off on the monitor and the whole house was dark.

"Well, if we are going to do it, we should probably go now," said Barkley, pointing a paw at the monitor. "Everybody's asleep."

"But what about our Curli and the Love Puppy Band?" asked Curli with a whine. "We were having so much fun singing to our faaaaaaaaans," she sang, holding the note.

"That'll have to wait," said Noodles.

Curli let out a huge sigh.

"Don't worry," said Noodles with a soft tone. "As soon as we finish this mission, we'll be back to wowing the teddy pups and bears all over the world. But right now, Magnolia needs us."

"Promise? As soon as you're done?" said Curli.

"Pretty Puppy Pinky Promise," said Noodles, reaching out her front paw.

"Pretty Puppy Pinky Promise," Curli said, touching her paw to Noodles's. "Well, there's no way I'm going back through that spinny thing, so I guess I'm going to bed. Good luck, Love Puppies. And good night." Curli blew a kiss and slouched off to Noodles's bedroom.

"It's now or never," reminded Barkley.

"Hold on," said Rosie. "We need a note!" She hurried over to a cabinet in the living room and pulled out a piece of paper and a pen. "No time for Typewriter-Barkley tonight. Puppy-penmanship will have to work!" After jotting down the note, Rosie folded it over and turned to face her team. "Okay, I'm ready."

With the magic words and their glowing paws in the middle, they opened the portal and jumped through.

* * *

The puppies landed outside Magnolia's sliding glass balcony door. But the door wasn't cracked this time—it was closed and locked. All the doors were locked. And all the windows on each of the sides of the house were, too.

"How are we supposed to get in?" asked Noodles.

"Maybe we can check the roof," answered Barkley. He changed his body into a small toy airplane and Rosie and Noodles climbed aboard. With Clyde beside them, they zipped up to the roof.

"Look!" said Clyde. "A window on the roof. And it's cracked open!"

"Paw-fect!" said Rosie.

The puppies carefully pushed the small window until it opened a bit more. They gazed down into the room.

"Yikes! That's quite a drop," said Rosie. "And I

don't think more than one of us can fit through at one time with how small this window is." She rubbed her chin for a moment and turned to look at Clyde and Barkley. "I think you boys should go, since you both can fly."

"We're on it!" responded Barkley.

"Remember: Find the diapers. Grab a stack and put them on Magnolia's desk with this note." Rosie handed Clyde the note. Her flowery handwriting spelled out:

> **Maggie,**
> **These are for you so you can help.**

Then Rosie had drawn a heart at the bottom.

"Definitely looks like her moms wrote that,"

said Noodles. "Nicely done, Rosie-Posie."

"Thanks," she said, a little pink reaching her cheeks. "You two ready to go?"

"Almost," said Barkley. His front legs began to stretch out and flatten, and feathers appeared. Then his head was replaced with a bird head and a beak. "H-owl do I look?" he asked, flapping his wings.

"Owl-some," said Clyde with a chuckle.

After squeezing through the window—with some pushes from Rosie and Noodles—Clyde and Owl-Barkley flew into the house. Inside, they soared silently near the high ceiling of the room.

"See any diapers?" whispered Owl-Barkley.

"Nope," responded Clyde. "This looks more like an office or something."

"Tryyyy the baaaaaby's roooom," came Noodles's voice on a slight breeze that swept through the office.

With that, the boys swooped out of the office door and down the hallway.

They checked one room: "No diapers here," whispered Clyde.

They checked the next room: "None here either," said Barkley.

Suddenly, they heard the soft sneeze of a baby.

"That way," mouthed Clyde.

With silent flight, Barkley and Clyde zoomed

into the baby's room. Soft music played and the air smelled like powder and flowers. A small night-light shined on the far wall and a monitor sat in the crib.

The two pups landed on the floor next to the crib and peered in. There was Baby Benji, lying on his back with his arms, legs, and body wrapped up snuggly in a baby blanket.

But just as they were looking at Benji, Benji was looking right back at them.

Oh no! Love Puppies are not supposed to be spotted by humans—had they been caught red-pawed?

Benji took a big breath and the boys braced themselves for his cry to shatter the silence.

Chapter 8
Diaper ~~Delivery~~ Disaster

Choo!

Benji sneezed another tiny baby sneeze and blinked his eyes as he stared at the pups.

"Gesundheit," said Barkley.

Then Benji yawned and made quiet baby noises.

"Aww," said Clyde. "He's sooo cute."

"Yes," said Barkley, changing back into his puppy body. "But he's got pipes like Curli. We've heard him cry. We'd better move quickly before this little guy starts yelling for his mamas."

The pups took two steps away from the crib. Benji cried out softly causing Barkley and Clyde to freeze. They turned and moved back toward his crib and Benji gurgled with delight.

"Uh-oh. I think he likes us," said Clyde.

"No problem," said Barkley. "You go find the diapers. I'll distract this little guy."

"Got it!"

"Want to see my moves?" whispered Barkley as

Benji watched quietly. "Here we go!" Barkley began

dancing back and forth, spinning and shimmying,

as he sang in a whispered voice:

"Hey, Benji, hey, Benji.

Wanna know a secret?

I can only tell you one.

I know the best way

that a Benji can have some fun.

You gotta

dance like nobaby's watching.

You gotta

sing like the world is your microphone.

You gotta

move and groove.

Hey! It's all up to you.

That's how a Benji has fun."

"Shake it, pup," whispered Clyde as he flew around the room in search of diapers.

Benji's eyes followed Barkley as he danced and sang. The baby's tiny body moved as if he were kicking and waving his arms inside the blanket.

Meanwhile, Clyde searched and searched. On top of tables. Inside baskets. Next to a framed picture of Maggie and her moms before Benji— they smiled so widely and looked so happy.

Clyde sighed. Maggie definitely was not happy like that anymore.

Finally, Clyde hurried over to a small cupboard

and opened the doors. Inside were the diapers.

"Found them," he whispered as Barkley continued to dance and sing for Benji.

Clyde grabbed a stack and zipped out of Benji's room and down the hall. He stopped at a slightly opened door and let his tummy shine just enough so he could read the sign on it:

Maggie's Room. No babies allowed.

"Yep. This is her room," he whispered to himself. He moved through the door quickly and placed the diapers on Maggie's bedside table with the note.

Back in the baby's room, Clyde said, "Diapers delivered. Let's get out of here."

"Bye, little Benji," whispered Barkley. He turned to leave, but Benji began fussing again.

"Oh yeah. He likes you for sure," said Clyde.

"Sorry, little guy. Gotta go. See ya." Barkley waved his paw and jumped onto Clyde's back.

As the two flew from Benji's room, the baby's cry rang out from his crib.

"Go, pup, go!" said Barkley. "We've only got a few seconds to make it out before Mom or Mommy come out to calm the screaming baby."

"Which room was it? Which room?" asked Clyde, panic in his voice. He flew this way and that through the darkened hallway.

"I don't remember," said Barkley.

"Was it this one?" he whispered, hovering next to a closed door.

Just then, the door opened and Barkley and Clyde were face-to-face with Mom.

"What on Earth?" she said, blinking and squinting.

Barkley moved fast, morphing into an invisible blanket and dropping over Clyde as Mom fumbled to put on her eyeglasses. She clicked the hallway light on and stared blankly into the space where the now-invisible pups floated.

"What is it?" called Mommy from inside the bedroom.

"I thought . . ." Mom began. "Nothing. Heading to Benji now."

By this time, Clyde and Barkley retraced their flight path and made their way back to the office with the high ceiling window. They zoomed out of it, almost knocking Rosie and Noodles backward.

"There you two are. How'd it go, Pups?" asked Rosie, startled by their hasty appearance.

Clyde and Barkley landed on the roof working to catch their breaths.

"Diapers placed right by her bed," said Clyde.

At that moment, they heard Maggie's voice blending in with Benji's cries.

"Diapers," she yelled. "Diapers to help? Are you serious. All you guys care about is that baby. What about me!" Maggie's voice called. "I don't want to help with diapers. I just want Benjamin Halverston to go away forever!"

The pups could hear something soft bounce off the wall of the hallway, and a door slammed.

Fast as lightning, the pups jumped onto Magic Carpet-Barkley's back and zipped around to Maggie's sliding glass door. By now, she was wide awake.

And the stack of diapers was no longer there.

The pups watched as she ripped up the note Rosie had written.

Did the Love Puppies just make matters worse?

Chapter 9
A Moment to Share

Rosie, Noodles, Barkley, and Clyde looked through Magnolia's sliding glass balcony door as she buried herself deep into her covers.

Her bedroom door opened and Mommy stepped in.

The pups held their breath. After what just happened, Maggie was sure to be in a whole lot of trouble.

Mommy walked over to the other side of the bed and sat down. She then reached out her hand and stroked Maggie's head through the covers.

Maggie's sobs grew louder, but Mommy's voice was soft.

"Having a new baby brother can be hard, huh?" said Mommy gently.

Maggie didn't reply.

Mommy continued on. "All the crying and feeding and crying and diapers. And crying. It can be a lot."

Maggie still did not say a word. Her head remained buried under her covers.

"It's been emotional for *us*, too. Me and your mom." Mommy paused for a moment, then said, "I'm going to share something that is really hard to say. I'm going to tell you because I think you deserve to know." Mommy took a deep, steadying breath. "I feel like I'm failing you, Mags. Like I'm failing you as a mommy."

At Mommy's words, Noodles's nose lit up brightly. A mixture of Mommy's emotions and Maggie's emotions—and some of her own.

"Your nose, pretty pup," Rosie called quietly. "Your nose. We'll be spotted."

Noodles took a deep breath, but it only dimmed some.

Mommy turned toward the darkened balcony window at the tiny spot of light. Quickly, Noodles moved her head and covered it with her paws. Mommy turned back toward Maggie who had stopped crying.

"That was close," Noodles said. "Sorry about that."

The pups hushed again and listened to Mommy who spoke.

"Seems like the fireflies are out tonight," she said with a small chuckle. "Anyway, I've been trying my best, Mags. And I know so much of our attention has been on Benji. He's a pretty challenging little guy with the colic and everything. But you know what, he *really* likes you. I can tell. He does this little kicking thing when he sees you."

"Really?" Maggie's muffled voice said from under the sheets. "You're not just saying that?"

"Really, really," Mommy said. "I know it doesn't seem like a lot, but he does. He just doesn't know how to show you how he feels yet." Mommy sat in silence a little longer. "So that's how I'm feeling. How are *you* feeling about all of this?"

The silence returned. Then, in a small voice, Maggie said, "I don't want to talk about it."

"Fair," said Mommy. "You don't have to talk

about it with me if you don't want to. But I am going to try to make sure I tell you more about how I'm feeling. That way, you can be comfortable sharing your feelings with me. Again. Like we used to."

Maggie still gave no answer.

Mommy leaned over and kissed the blanket that still covered Maggie's head. "Even though it may not feel like it, we are here. And you are always loved. *Always*. You're our best girl. I'm here when you are ready to talk."

Mommy stood and took a few steps toward the door. "Good night, Mags. I love you." This was followed by more silence.

But when Mommy shut the door, Maggie whispered: "I love you, Mommy."

"I think it's time to call it a night," said Rosie. "We've got a lot to think about so we can help Maggie through this tough situation—without making it any worse."

With that, the pups hurried back through the Doggie Door portal. But each of them felt more and more unsure about what to do next to help.

Chapter 10
Sing a Song with Feeling

When the Love Puppies returned to the Doghouse,

a sad, slow melody reached their ears.

"All alone, all alone

Who will be there to love me?

All alone, all alone

Who is there thinking of me?

Sometimes a girl

needs a friend in her world.

Who will be that friend

For me?"

The beautiful song floated down the hall from Noodles's room and right to each puppy's eardrums. And the Love Puppies burst into whimpering sobs and huddled together in a heap.

The song stopped and Curli's footsteps could be heard padding down the hallway.

"You're back!" she said excitedly with a huge smile on her face and a sparkly, teal-colored notebook in her paw. But when she found them, they were a puddle of puppy tears.

"I'm sorry," cried Noodles. "I'm not being a good host *and* we're failing Maggie." A rain cloud formed quickly above her and a drizzle of raindrops bounced off her head, illuminated by her glowing nose.

"We didn't mean to make you feel so sad," sobbed Clyde.

"We were just trying to complete our mission," cried Barkley, "and it's been so very hard!"

"Calm down, Pups," said Curli. "I'm okay. I was just working on a new song. It's called 'Needing a Friend.' I was feeling pretty sad you guys were gone—but I'm okay. See?!" She flipped open a page of her notebook and showed them some songs she wrote. "Some are sad songs. Some are happy. I write songs when I'm feeling blue or joyful—or anywhere in the middle."

She flipped the page to the song she taught them the other night. "See. No tears here. Just pretty songs."

The pups calmed their whimpering, though the sad song still rang in their ears.

"I know what can cheer you up," Curli said.

"Hey, puppies, hey, puppies.

Wanna know a secret?

I can only tell you one . . ."

She continued singing, twirling and dancing this way and that. As she sang, happiness seemed to flow from her.

In no time, the pups were back to smiling, dancing, and joining in on her song. Even Noodles twirled and sang.

"See," said Curli once the song was finished, "writing songs helps me when I'm having a whole bunch of emotions. Whether happy, sad, or annoyed," she said, fluffing the fur on Noodles's cheek. "I've got a bunch of songs here inspired by my sisters, brothers . . . and cousins." She winked at Noodles and laughed. "Then I practice singing them, and it helps me feel better. It's whaaaat I doooooo," she sang.

Noodles could relate. When her pet caterpillar, Pearla Ray, had flown away after transforming into a butterfly, writing a song had definitely made her feel better. Especially when she shared the song with her puppy pals.

Just then, her nose blinked like an idea light bulb flashing above someone's head.

"Curli, you just gave me a great idea!" said Noodles. "Maggie wasn't ready to talk to Mommy about her thoughts. So, maybe *that's* what she needs! A journal or notebook to write down all her feelings!"

"Yes!" said Rosie. "That's a pup-riffic idea!"

"I have an extra one," said Curli. "I bring two

just in case I run out of pages. But you are more than welcome to give the other one to Maggie. She needs it more than me today. Wait right here!"

Curli dashed from the living room to Noodles's room where her bags were. When she came back with the blank notebook in her teeth, she handed it over to Noodles. Rosie then stuck a new note right on top: *For your thoughts and feelings.*

"Clyde and Barkley," began Noodles, "since you know the house better than us, will you do the honor of dropping off this notebook?"

"You've got it!" said Clyde with a flying flip.

The puppies opened the portal and Clyde flew in with invisible Blanket-Barkley over him. Clyde held the notebook and note in his teeth as he soared. The other pups positioned themselves right in front of the Mission Monitor to watch the boys in action.

"Nothing yet," said Noodles as the monitor continued to focus in on Maggie sleeping.

A moment later, a little Clydie face poked out from thin air next to Maggie's bedside table. He carefully placed the note and book. Then he waved, knowing the other pups could see him.

"Hi there, Clydie," Rosie said with a giggle as she, Curli, and Noodles waved back happily at the screen. They knew he couldn't hear or see them, but they couldn't help but wave.

* * *

Clyde vanished, back under the safety of Barkley-Blanket's invisible shield. Rosie, Noodles, and Curli hurried away from the monitor and back to the open portal. There they waited . . . and waited.

And waited.

"They should be back by now, right?" asked Curli.

"They did already put the notebook down. Where are they?" asked Rosie, her eyebrows crinkling with concern.

"You don't think the window got shut, do you?" asked Noodles, her nose glowing with worry. "What if they are stuck in there forever?" The feeling of guilt returned to Noodles as she thought about the time Barkley almost got locked into a kid's bedroom when he morphed into a frog during a previous mission. That had been because of one of her ideas then, too.

"Bone," said Rosie, "please show us the roof window."

Sure enough, the window was sealed tightly. Water drips from rainfall had collected on the glass.

One of the moms must have closed it.

"Oh no! What are we going to do?" howled Noodles.

How in the world would Rosie, Noodles, and Curli be able to get their puppy pals out of there now?

Chapter 11
A Moment in the Spotlight

Rosie and Noodles paced back and forth across the living room floor in front of the Mission Monitor. How were they going to retrieve their locked-in pups?

"What if we go in through a chimney or something?" asked Rosie.

"I don't remember seeing one big enough to fit a puppy," said Noodles. "And neither of us can fly, so how would we get down it safely?"

"Good point," Rosie said, her puppy feet still padding back and forth across the room.

"Should we try breaking a window?" asked Curli.

"I really don't think that's a good idea," said Rosie. "We try not to bring any harm to the human world."

Noodles scratched her head. "I can't think of *anything*," she said, panicked. "What if they are stuck in there forever and ever and ever and it's all *my* fault?!"

"Don't worry about that, pretty pup," said Rosie,

hugging her friend. "I know we'll be able to get them out of there. We just have to figure out the right how."

"Hmmmm," said Curli, scrunching up her face in thought. "Maybe we can sing right outside the window so one of the moms will open up the door, and then we all rush inside!"

"I don't know how we'd do that without being seen," said Rosie.

"You can't be seen by humans?" asked Curli.

"Not as Love Puppies," answered Noodles. "It will delay our mission and may impact our magic. We've only been seen by two human girls, but it was okay because they bonded as our forever friends."

"Well, since I'm not a Love Puppy," said Curli, "*I* can be seen. And I like to be," she said, flipping her lovely poodle curls.

"It's worth a try!" said Noodles, perked up by the idea. "Let's go—wait, but you hate the Doggie Door portal," reminded Noodles.

"I think I can stomach one more adventure if it means helping those pooch-pals. They're just like brothers to me," Curli said.

"Then let's go!" called Rosie.

The three girls jumped back through the portal that was still open from when the boys left. When they made it to the human world, the sun was already beginning to rise in the sky. It had truly been a long night for the team of magical puppies.

Still a little shaky, Curli took a deep breath and closed her eyes.

"You good, Curli-Girly?" asked Noodles.

Curli opened her eyes and nodded. "I'm ready for my close-up!"

Curli strode out across the lawn and positioned herself near the porch. Rosie and Noodles watched from their hideaway spot behind a large bush on the right side of the house.

Then Curli opened her mouth and began to sing.

Loud, bold, and beautiful!

Though words came out for the puppies to hear, only beautiful howls reached the human ears. Her notes brought tears to Rosie's and Noodles's eyes.

Curli continued to sing with all her might, putting emotion into every note. It was as if she stood on an opera stage in New York City or Sydney, Australia. She sang and sang and sang.

The front door of Maggie's house opened. Mom peered outside. Then the door opened all the way up, and there stood the whole family: Mommy holding Benji, and Magnolia beside her. The family seemed to be captivated by the random dog howling beautifully on their front lawn.

Mommy put her arm around Magnolia and laid her head on her head. Mom put her arm around Mommy.

Curli sang with her eyes closed as if she were entranced by her own song.

And right between the tops of Mommy's and Mom's heads and the threshold of the door, Clyde and Barkley came sailing through. They went completely unnoticed by anyone except for Benji, who giggled as he watched them soar away.

Curli hit her last note and stopped. She stared at the family, took a bow, and then blew a kiss.

Then she bolted to the bush where the other puppies waited, and within a blink of a puppy eye, Curli and the Love Puppies disappeared into the Doggie Door portal—just in time!

Chapter 12
Words to Share

Safely home at the Doghouse and beneath the fluttering fabric of the excited banner-puppies, Rosie, Noodles, and Curli jumped on and hugged Barkley and Clyde.

"We are so happy you are safe!" said

Noodles, kissing each of their cheeks.

"We were so worried," said Curli.

"And it's all thanks to Curli's amazing voice!" said Rosie.

"Look," said Curli, now facing the Mission Monitor, "they are still at it."

The puppies watched as Maggie and her moms, plus Benji in Mommy's arms, ran around the yard in their pajamas, looking behind each bush. They checked behind the house, baskets, and bins.

Mom rubbed her head in confusion as Mommy hugged Benji. "That beautiful, howling dog was real, right?" asked Mom.

Maggie and Mommy nodded their heads.

"So, I'm not the only one who saw and heard that. I didn't imagine the whole thing?"

"Oh, we definitely saw it, too, hun," said Mommy.

"Then how could a whole dog that was here three minutes ago now be absolutely gone?"

Mommy shrugged her shoulders.

"It would have been nice to have a pet puppy," said Maggie.

Just then, Maggie grabbed a pile of leaves and tossed them at Mom. Mom laughed and did the same back to her—which led to a leaf fight filled with laughter and love.

"Look!" said Rosie.

Maggie grabbed a leaf and playfully wiggled it

at Benji. He laughed and kicked his legs. Then he blew bubbles with his lips.

"See. I told you he loves you," said Mommy. "He's blowing you a Benji kiss."

The family laughed some more, and Maggie leaned over and kissed his cheek. Benji clapped.

And the puppies yipped with delight as they watched the family heading back inside, arm in arm.

"Bone, take us inside, please," said Rosie.

The Monitor blinked and then they saw both moms sitting with Benji on a couch in the living room.

"Where'd Maggie go?" asked Noodles. She was sure that the family strife had been squashed with their joyful fun outside.

Maggie hurried into the living room, holding a journal. She stopped in front of her mothers and opened it.

"She used it?" asked Curli. With the commotion of rescuing Barkley and Clyde, the pups had missed that Maggie had not only opened Curli's notebook but had written some things inside.

"Can I share something with you?" Maggie asked.

"Of course," said Mom.

"Okay, here it goes:

Sad filled my heart up

when the new baby came home.

He did not like me.

Oh, how my heart felt broken

cold and alone with no home."

Mom, Mommy, and Benji listened quietly as Magnolia read.

"That was beautiful," said Mommy. "I didn't know you wrote poetry."

"It's called a tanka", Magnolia said, smiling proudly. "It means 'a short song' in Japanese. My teacher taught it to us in school."

"It was amazing. Thanks for sharing your feelings with us," said Mom.

"And look how much Benji listened when you read. He's never that quiet when *I* read him anything," said Mommy.

"Or when I do," agreed Mom.

"Maybe that could be a Maggie job. If you like," said Mommy. "Reading bedtime poems and stories to us all. Ones you write. Ones you like. I know how much you love to read!"

"There is this one book I love to read aloud to myself. Maybe Benji would like it, too?" Maggie looked down at her shoes, then back up at her moms. "I'd like that Maggie job."

"That would be so much help!" said Mommy. "Come here, Mommy's special girl," she said, opening her arms.

"You haven't called me that in, like, forever," said Maggie as she sat between Mom and Mommy. Both parents embraced her.

"You're right. It has been a while since I called you that," said Mommy.

"How about this," added Mom. "Let's have Benji visit Aunt Vivian on Saturday, and the three of us can go on an outing together. Just you, Mommy, and me. Anywhere you want to go, Mags."

"Really?" asked Maggie.

"We'll make a routine out of it," said Mom. "So each night, Maggie reads a story, and each week, we have some Mags-Mommy-Mom time."

"I really like that idea!" said Maggie.

Both moms kissed Maggie on a separate cheek and her smile glowed as brightly as Noodles's nose did as she and the other pups watched this special family moment play out on the Mission Monitor screen.

Noodles took a deep breath and then sang a little song to herself, *"Calm, calm, calm, and low. Help me cool and dim my glow."* Noodles sang it to herself two more times, and finally, her nose dimmed completely.

"You did it, pup," said Rosie.

"Deep breaths help," said Noodles, "but a good song seemed to do the trick. I learned that from my favorite cousin!"

"Aww," said Curli. "Music is like a miracle."

Chapter 13
The Best Guest

"You gotta

dance like nopuppy's watching.

You gotta

sing like the world is your microphone.

You gotta

move and groove.

Hey! It's all up to you.

That's how a puppy has fuuuuuun!"

Curli and the Love Puppies sang as loudly as their little puppy lungs allowed. They danced and swayed through the living room and the banner-pups yipped and grooved on their fabric.

After the song was done, they all fell into a puppy pile laughing wildly.

"We're so glad you came to visit," said Noodles.

"At first, I didn't think you were, cousin," said Curli. "You guys were so focused on your mission and I felt left out. I totally let my emotions get the best of me."

"Yeah, that definitely happens," said Rosie. "Like Magnolia did with the new baby. I wonder how she's doing now." Rosie activated her chest heart, and within it, the pups could see Magnolia sitting snuggled up next to Mom and Mommy and Benji—Maggie held a bedtime story and read it aloud.

"Seems as if she finally feels like she fits back in with the family," said Clyde.

"Being left out does hurt," said Curli. "Especially when you are used to something else, like Noodly-Doodly giving me all her attention."

"True. But when you were feeling bad, you figured out a way to get your feelings out. You wrote them

115

down and sang them out loud," said Noodles.

"Instead of keeping them bottled up," said Barkley. "That's not a good thing to do."

"Righto, Barkley Boy," said Rosie. "But you also can't blow up with anger either. It's all about taking deep breaths, figuring out what you are feeling, and telling others—whether it's through talking, speaking, drawing, writing poetry, or even singing."

"I do admit, I felt like I barely got any of your attention when I first got here. I definitely felt all alone," Curli said, a sad look on her face. "Kinda like how I do at home when my mommy and daddy are giving my crazy puplings all their attention.

That's part of the reason they decided to let me come visit here."

"We never meant to make you feel like that," said Noodles, petting her cousin's soft fur.

"But once I saw how Maggie was feeling—and could completely relate—I wanted to try to be helpful. You know, by giving you pups ideas. And also, by giving you a chance to sing and dance and burn off some steam when you were feeling low."

"Like you did that first night when we were all sad. You taught us your song and it *really* helped," said Barkley. "But it didn't just help *us* feel better, it even helped Benji."

"Yep," said Clyde. "Barkley sang your song to him and did a dance that kept him quiet while we were delivering the diapers."

"You did?" said Curli. "I didn't know that."

"And come to think about it—whose idea was the diapers in the first place?" asked Clyde.

"Mine," said Curli. "But it was a total fail."

"We have fails all the time," said Rosie, "but that doesn't stop us."

"It was also your idea to give Magnolia a journal to capture her thoughts," said Noodles. "We didn't even know she'd capture her *own* talent of writing poems in it while helping her get her emotions out. That was all you."

"You're pup-tastic!" said Rosie. "You were more help than you even knew!"

"And nopup will ever forget how your beautiful voice helped bring that family back together once again. Magic is nothing when you have talent like yours. Your voice has the power to make others feel amazing," said Noodles.

"Yeah. I guess you are all right. Here, I was thinking I didn't fit in, but it turns out, I was helping more than I even knew by just being me and sharing the things that I know and am good at," said Curli.

"Just like Magnolia. Even though having a new sibling is hard, big puplings can always find ways to help by being themselves, understanding how they are feeling, and sharing those feelings in a healthy way," said Rosie.

"Curli-Girly, you have been the best guest we've ever had," said Noodles, "and we've loved having you."

After a Clyde-prepared dinner, the pups gathered near the front door.

"Well, it's time for me to go since my vacation is over," said Curli. She hugged each pup. "But thank you for letting me be myself and for giving me a chance to help you on your mission. It has truly been amaaaaaazing," sang Curli.

"You are welcome back anytime," said Rosie.

At that, the pups all jumped on Curli and covered her in more kisses.

Feeling like you belong and feeling loved by those who are special to you really makes for a magically pup-tastic vacation away. Don't you think?

Read all of the Love Puppies' paw-some adventures!